THE
Silly OZbuls
OF OZ

ROGER S. BAUM

ILLUSTRATED BY
LISA MERTINS

Yellow Brick Road
Publishers, Inc.
California

Library of Congress Catalog Card Number 91-66003
ISBN 0-9630101-0-7

Dedicated to

Charlene
My Wife. My Friend.
We share an adventure.

ROGER

To My Daughter Jordan
Who has taken me with her
many times on her trips to Oz.

LISA

In Memory Of
Alicia Denise Backstrom
Resting where rainbows
are made.

R.B.

Preface

SillyOZbuls have round, cuddly, furry, pink bodies, on top of one spring-like leg with a large flat foot. The big toe is pointed upward and all the rest of their toes pointed downward.

Their neck is a spring, just like their leg. Attached to the neck is a furry round head. The head has two sleepy eyes; the eyes are round with the eyelids shaped like they're half closed and half not closed. You cannot see a mouth because of all the pink fur. But, you can see a small moustache. Also, they have two small devilish looking horns on the top of their heads.

The SillyOZbuls are full of love and many citizens of Oz cuddle and play with them.

SillyOZbuls are disappearing from Oz. There are only five SillyOZbuls left, when there used to be hundreds. Every week, the ground rumbles, and another cuddly SillyOZbul disappears. Where do they disappear to? Maybe, they just vanish forever. Something has to be done to save them.

A Munchkin by the name of Dom, became very worried when his SillyOZbul disappeared. Dom decided to travel down the Yellow Brick Road to visit the Wizard of Oz at the Emerald City, just as Dorothy and her little dog Toto did years ago. Perhaps, the good Wizard could save the SillyOZbuls.

The SillyOZbuls of OZ

After traveling down the Yellow Brick Road awhile, Dom met a funny-looking bird called a Wiser. It had a large forehead and two big round eyes. It's neck looked like a rope. He had a small round body and two bird-like claws protruded. Wiser looked somewhat like an owl and was very wise.

"Where are you going?" asked Wiser, in his usual wise matter-of-fact voice.

"I am going to see the Wizard of Oz at the Emerald City," said Dom. "My SillyOZbul has disappeared."

"I know all about the SillyOZbuls," said the wise Wiser. "I know how cuddly and full of love they are. That is exactly their problem."

"What do you mean, 'their problem'? Being cuddly and full of love cannot be a problem. Can it?" asked Dom.

"For a SillyOZbul it is," said Wiser. "I will explain. Once every thousand years, a very powerful and Evil Wizard comes to Oz to take away something that is special to people. *Now* is that time. The Evil Wizard has cast a spell upon the SillyOZbuls.

"If the spell is not reversed, there will not be any SillyOZbuls left and that will make him very, very happy. And it will make everyone else very, very sad. Which in turn, will make the Evil Wizard even happier. You see," said Wiser, "the Evil Wizard wants everyone to be miserable for another thousand years."

"Then I must continue my journey to the Emerald
City and ask the Good Wizard of Oz for help," said Dom.

Wiser thought a moment, "There are only four SillyOZbuls left in Oz. You will never make it to the Emerald City in time to save them. Maybe you can ask the Scarecrow. He is close to the Yellow Brick Road and not nearly as far as the Emerald City. The Scarecrow has a wonderful brain, that the Wizard of Oz gave him. Maybe he can tell you how to break the Evil Wizard's spell. He has a lot more experience in these things than I do."

"Thank you for your information and concern. I will ask the Scarecrow," said Dom.

"Please say hello to him for me," said Wiser. "Good luck," he added, as he flew away.

It wasn't much further down the Yellow Brick Road when Dom came across the Scarecrow trying to scare away some crows.

"Excuse me, Scarecrow. My name is Dom and I desperately need your advice. Wiser said maybe you could help."

"Wiser!" shouted the Scarecrow. "I'm not much at scaring crows and the Wiser Bird doesn't scare at all. Maybe it's because he is very intelligent," admitted the Scarecrow. "How can I help?"

Dom told the Scarecrow about what was happening to all the SillyOZbuls.

"The spell must be broken," agreed the Scarecrow.

"First," said the Scarecrow, "let's go back to where you last saw your SillyOZbul."

Together, they left the cornfield and walked back along the Yellow Brick Road to Dom's home.

On the way, Wiser flew overhead and wished them well. "Be careful," said Wiser. "The Evil Wizard has gone to the East of Oz for now, but he could be back soon."

"Thank you for your information," said the Scarecrow.

"We must work fast." said the Scarecrow. "If the Evil Wizard thought we were trying to foil him, who knows what he might do."

Later, they were back at Dom's home. It was night. "You must be tired," said the Scarecrow, "and it is late. Since I don't require any sleep, I'll just stand and think."

All through the night, while Dom slept, the Scarecrow thought with the brain the Wizard of Oz gave him. He thought and thought and by morning he had an idea.

When Dom woke, the Scarecrow asked if there was a dollmaker in the village.

"Yes," said Dom, "Her name is Garla."

"I have an idea on how to break the spell," answered the Scarecrow. "But first, we must visit Garla to see if she can help."

That morning they went to her toy shop. Inside, there were dragon dolls, toy soldiers even Dorothy and Toto dolls. There were all kinds of dolls.

The Scarecrow was startled to find a Scarecrow doll. "Everyone in Oz knows you," said Garla. "I made it in your honor."

"I am indeed honored," said the Scarecrow. "Thank you, Garla."

The Scarecrow asked the dollmaker if she had ever seen a SillyOZbul?

"Oh my, yes," answered Garla. "I have enjoyed watching Dom play with his SillyOZbul."

"Do you think you could create a life-size SillyOZbul costume for Dom?" asked the Scarecrow.

The dollmaker didn't hesitate. "Why, of course I can make the costume. It would be fun."

"And it may be difficult," added the Scarecrow. "The costume must look like a real SillyOZbul. Dom will be inside of it. The Evil Wizard must not know the difference. When the Evil Wizard tries to cast his spell on Dom, he will not disappear. The Evil Wizard's spell will have no effect."

"What will the Evil Wizard do?" asked Dom.

"We will see," said the Scarecrow. "We will see."

Again the ground rumbled.

Another Munchkin named Zeb, who was the town's watchmaker and a good friend of Garla's, ran into the doll shop shouting, "My SillyOZbul is gone!"

"We must hurry! There are only three SillyOZbuls left. In three weeks, all the remaining SillyOZbuls will be gone and so will the Evil Wizard. He will be gone for another thousand years," added the Scarecrow.

SillyOZbuls of OZ

Garla, the dollmaker, started her work immediately. She measured Dom for his costume.

"Because SillyOZbuls have one spring-like leg and neck, Dom will have to be entirely inside the costume's torso. Except, your arms will be inside its arms," said the dollmaker. "I will make two eyeholes under its fur for you to see out."

"I can make the spring-like neck and leg," said Zeb, the Watchmaker. "At the top of the leg, I will put a bar with two footholds. The bar and the footholds will be inside the costume. The Evil Wizard will not know the difference."

The work of making the SillyOZbul costume began in earnest.

The earth shook again. Now, there were only two SillyOZbuls.

Working quickly, the watchmaker finished the SillyOZbul's spring-like neck and leg.

Dom put a cloth sack over himself with two eyeholes cut out, to simulate the SillyOZbul costume and began to practice moving about by bouncing up and down on the leg and foot that Zeb had made him. Dom fell over again and again but, he didn't give up. He had to succeed. Each time he fell, he would remember his cuddly friend who gave him so much love that he immediately got up and practiced again.

All the while, Garla worked to finish the SillyOZbul costume. In three days, the SillyOZbul's head with it's sleepy eyes and tiny horns were finished.

When Dom saw the head, he became very quiet, "It looks just like my SillyOZbul."

The ground shook hard again.

"Does that mean another SillyOZbul has disappeared?" asked Zeb.

"I'm afraid it does," answered the Scarecrow. "Now we have one week to get ready or it will be too late."

Dom practiced and practiced with his spring-like SillyOZbul leg. Finally, Dom yelled from beneath his funny looking cloth sack, "Look everyone! I can do it! I can move about just like my SillyOZbul."

The Scarecrow, Garla and Zeb clapped and roared with laughter. As serious as the situation was, it was very funny watching the cloth sack, with Dom inside, bouncing from one end of the room to the other. Dom had also learned to balance himself perfectly still on the spring's big foot. "Congratulations," said the Scarecrow.

Garla worked feverishly to complete the rest of the SillyOZbul costume. The most difficult part was the pink fur that needed to be sewn to the costume's body.

As she worked, the Scarecrow, Dom and Zeb kept her company during the long tedious hours.

Finally, the costume's head, neck, leg and foot were attached to the body.

SillyOZbuls of OZ

There were just two days left before the last SillyOZbul would disappear along with the Evil Wizard.

Dom climbed inside the SillyOZbul costume. There, before everyone's eyes, was a pink and cuddly SillyOZbul.

Dom bounced up and down. All his practice paid off. It was perfect.

"Tomorrow, there will be one day remaining," said the Scarecrow. "Tomorrow will be the big day."

That night, no one could sleep. They spent the night planning their strategy.

At dawn they were on their way to the town square to the very place where Dorothy and Toto began their trip to the Emerald City years ago.

It was early. No one was in the square except the four of them.

Zeb and Dom, in his SillyOZbul costume, pretended to play, while Garla and the Scarecrow hid, out of sight.

The earth shook harder than it ever shook before. Many Munchkins in town rushed to their doors.

SillyOZbuls of OZ

The last SillyOZbul in Oz had disappeared. There was a strange silence. Then, the ground shook again. And there in front of everyone's eyes stood the Evil Wizard. He was dressed in black including his black cape and hat. His eyes were as black as coal. From the wand in his hand came forth bolts of lightning and storm clouds blocked out the morning sunlight.

The Evil Wizard looked so terrible that Dom, in his SillyOZbul costume, almost lost his balance but, continued to bounce up and down. Zeb just stood, frozen in fear.

The Evil Wizard roared, "What is this? How could I have missed a SillyOZbul? It is time for me to leave Oz for another thousand years but I cannot leave until I have caused all SillyOZbuls to disappear!"

With that, the Evil Wizard raised his Wand and said, "I hate all creatures that give love and SillyOZbuls give love. Away, last remaining SillyOZbul!" A bolt of lightning flashed from the Evil Wizard's wand. "Away and disappear forever!" he screamed.

Nothing happened. Dom, in his costume stood perfectly still. The Wizard screamed his spell again, "Away love! Away and disappear, last remaining SillyOZbul!"

SillyOZbuls of OZ

The ground shook again and the Munchkins who came to their doors, closed and bolted them.

Again, as before, stood the SillyOZbul with Zeb by his side. The Evil Wizard stepped closer to them and said, "I must rid Oz of all SillyOZbuls because they give so much love. Why don't you disappear, SillyOZbul, as all the others?" The Wizard looked at his wand, as if something was wrong with its evil power.

The Wizard's eyes flashed in hate. Just then, Dom in his cuddly SillyOZbul costume, bounced high in the air toward the Wizard. Dom grabbed the Wizard and gave him a big furry, lovable hug. Zeb ran over and also hugged the Evil Wizard.

"No one in thousands and thousands of years has ever loved me. It cannot be true. Why do you not disappear like the others?" The Evil Wizard was completely fooled.

"Time has run out!" he screamed. "I must leave now! I must return to where love is not and evil reigns. If SillyOZbuls and people like you, Zeb, have that much love for each other, perhaps I have been wrong. My spell is broken."

The ground shook again. The Evil Wizard was gone. But there, filling the whole town square were hundreds of pink, furry and lovable SillyOZbuls, all anxious to go back to the people they love.

The Scarecrow and Garla ran towards Zeb and Dom and gave them big SillyOZbul hugs.

"It just goes to show what love can do," said the Scarecrow.

SPECIAL THANK YOU

To Tim and Jill Murch